Mimi's Book of Opposites

Emma Chichester Clark

ini Charlesbridge

My baby brother
is SMALL
and I am
BIG.

He is NAUGHTY and I am GOOD.

I say, "YES!"
but he says,
"NO!"

I swing him
HIGH . . .

I swing him
LOW.

UP . . .

DOWN . . .

UP!

DOWN . . .

When we
COME,
we say, *"HELLO."*

When we GO,
we wave
GOODBYE.

Sometimes we are WET.
Sometimes we are DRY.

I push him FAST.
I push him SLOW.

He gets *DIRTY*
all *DAY*,

but he gets *CLEAN* at NIGHT.

In his bath he LAUGHS.

When he gets out
he CRIES.

We OPEN the window.
His eyes are SHUT tight.